THIS

SWEET PICKLES ®

BOOK BELONGS TO

In the Town of Sweet Pickles, the animals get into and out of pickles because of their all too human personality traits.

Each of the books in the *Sweet Pickles* series is about a different pickle.

This book is about swimming lessons.

Library of Congress Cataloging in Publication Data

Hefter, Richard.
    Wet all over.
    (Sweet Pickles)
    SUMMARY: While all the other animals of Sweet Pickles
are learning to swim, Vain Vulture is interested only in
showing off his new bathing suit.
    [1. Swimming—Fiction.   2. Price and vanity—Fiction.
3. Animals—Fiction]   I. Title.
PZ7.H3587We   [E]   81-9879
ISBN 0-937524-12-3   AACR2

Weekly Reader Books Presents

WET ALL OVER

Written and illustrated
by Richard Hefter
Edited by Ruth Lerner Perle

Euphrosyne Incorporated

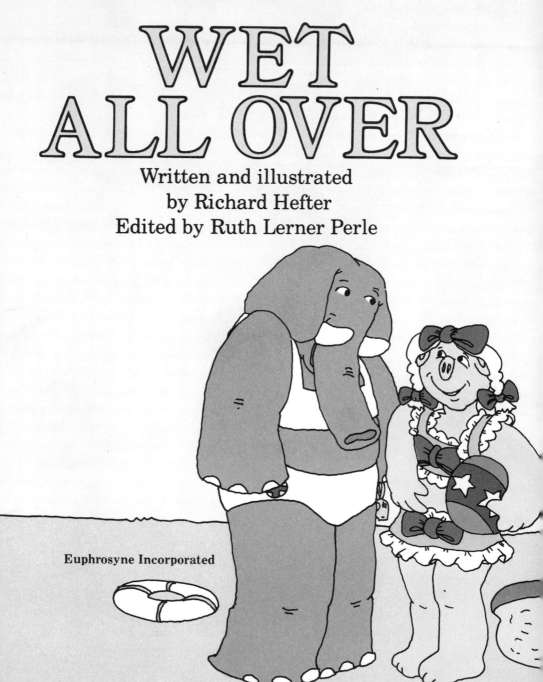

It was a hot summer day in the Town of Sweet Pickles.

Enormous Elephant was down at the pond with Positive Pig.

"I'm going to start the swimming lessons," said Elephant, "just as soon as the others get here."

Worried Walrus came walking down the path with Moody Moose and Loving Lion.

"I brought my blow-up water wings," said Walrus.
"And an extra towel and some suntan oil and a first
  aid kit ... just in case."

"Let's get started!" smiled Lion.

"I always wanted to learn how to swim," said Moose.

"First," lectured Elephant, "you have to know about the rules. Everyone must listen to what I say. When you hear me blow my whistle, stop whatever you are doing and hold up your hands."

"O K ," they all said.

Just then, Vain Vulture came walking down the path to the edge of the pond. He spread a big towel on the dock and propped his mirror up on it. He sat down and held his sun reflector up under his chin. Then, he leaned back to face the sun.

"Would you like to join the group?" asked Elephant. "I'm giving a swimming lesson so that everyone can learn about water safety."

"Swimming lesson!" sneered Vulture. "For me? I don't need any swimming lessons. Just look at this body. I'm a natural athlete. Besides, I just came down here to get a tan...and to show you my terrific new designer bathing ensemble. See? Everything is color coordinated."

Elephant turned back to the group and continued with the lesson. She asked everyone to get into the water at the shallow end.

"Now remember," said Elephant, " hands up when you hear the whistle."

"Ha, ha!" jeered Vulture. "How can you swim with your hands up? I never heard of anything so silly. You look perfectly ridiculous!"

"And," exclaimed Elephant, "we are going to use the buddy system. Everyone, choose a buddy and stay together while you are swimming. That's water safety."

"That's water dummies!" laughed Vulture from the dock. "Now you have to swim in pairs." Vulture leaned back and looked deeply into his mirror. "I would never swim in pairs," he said. "I could never find anybody as wonderful as I am to be *my* buddy."

Lion chose Moose for a buddy. Walrus chose Pig. Elephant showed them how to kick their feet. Everybody splished and splashed.

"Watch out!" exclaimed Vulture. "You splashed me and my swim suit almost got wet!"

Next, Elephant taught them how to stroke with their arms and how to breathe.

"This is great!" exclaimed Pig. "This is wonderful!"

"Be careful," cautioned Walrus. "Don't go too fast."

"Wheee!" squealed Moose. "I'm swimming!"

"I love it!" sputtered Lion. "I just love it!"

Everyone swam back and forth and back and forth.
They splished and sploshed and had a wonderful
time while Elephant watched over them.

"Hmphh!" sneered Vulture. "I'm glad *I* don't need any swimming lessons. I'm happy *I* don't have to listen to Elephant." Vulture stood up, put on his sun hat, and paraded around the edge of the pond.

"You there!" shouted Vulture. "Have you seen my fantastic new bathing suit? Hey, Walrus, I'm talking to you!"

But Walrus was too busy swimming. So were Pig and Lion and Moose.

Nobody paid any attention to Vulture at all.

"How can they appreciate my new bathing suit if they won't even stop to look at it properly?" grumbled Vulture.

Vulture walked over to Elephant and grabbed the whistle from her.

"Hey!" cried Elephant. "You can't do that! I'm the lifeguard and that's my whistle!"

"I'm only going to borrow it for a minute," laughed Vulture, as he ran over to the very edge of the dock.

"TWEEEEEEEEEEEEEEEEEEEEEEEEET!" Vulture blew the whistle as loudly as he could.

Everybody stopped still in the water and held up their arms.

"Now listen to me!" shouted Vulture. "This is important!" He moved closer to the edge of the dock and stood on tip-toe so that they could all see him. "I want you all to look at my new bathing suit. Isn't it gorgeous?"

Vulture started to turn around to show off the back of his suit. His foot slipped and he began to wave his arms.

"HELP!" cried Vulture as he fell off the dock. "I'm falling in!"

Vulture landed in the water with a gigantic
SPLASH! Elephant dove in to rescue him. All the
others swam over to help.

They towed Vulture back to shore and sat him down at the edge of the water. He was sputtering and coughing.

"Don't worry," said Walrus. "We'll help you."

"We'll teach you," smiled Lion. "I'll be your buddy."

"Never!" sniffed Vulture. "Just look at me! You and your swimming lessons have ruined my new swim suit. Look at it! It's wet all over!"

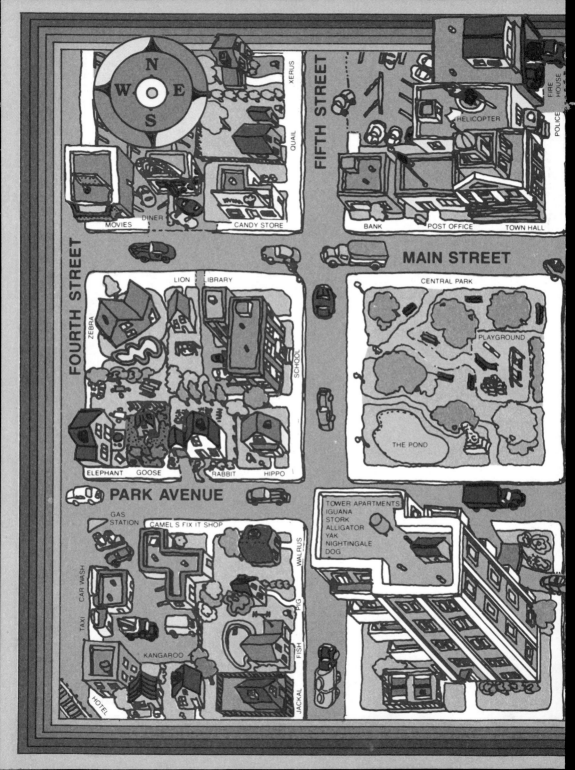